Ada

Jacqueline Signori

Library of Congress Cataloging-in-Publication Data

Signori, Jacqueline

Ada / Jacqueline Signori

ISBN 978-0-6151-8518-7

DEDICATION

This novella is dedicated to the wagers of peace everywhere.
You know who you are.

ACKNOWLEDGEMENTS

I would like to thank many people for the encouragement and hands-on help they gave to me in the course of my writing.

First, my sister, Carol, who made it possible for me to enter graduate school when I did and so led to the completion of this novella. Her children, Anne, Elizabeth, and Margaret (in alphabetical order) who always believed in me.

Second, three young women who typed one of my first manuscripts in the early 1990's and they are as follows: Johanna Cornette, Margaret Rosa, and Anya Hoerlein.

Third, all my writing group co-members throughout the many years of our writing, and they are as follows:

Gloria, Cheryl, Linda, Corinne, Amalia, Elinor, Mary, Judith, Rae, Karla, all of Rae and Karla's students through the years, Laurence, Francesca, Sheila; all of us at Sallee's who are at various times the following: Sallee, Sharon, Toni, Marcia, Jasmine, Caroline, Brianna, Mary Ellen, Kathy, Carol, Cielle, Deborah. (I hope I did not forget anyone.)

Meg, who deserves a line of her own, and is my first reader.

All my graduate school readers, you know who you are.

The International Women's Writing Guild.

To all my colleagues at Kirkwood Community College, who make the environment conducive to creativity.

To all my students who keep me from complacency.

To everyone who works, or has worked at The Fairfield Public Library.

To all my great elementary school teachers, most importantly, John.

To Jeff, who puts up with it all.

Prologue

Ada saw Tom, tall and lean, standing on the porch, wearing his favorite cotton sweater and khaki slacks. She wondered how he could tolerate the early summer heat in those clothes. She wore as little as possible, seersucker shorts and a sleeveless blouse, and stood barefoot on the shady concrete stoop. "I've been thinking about you, and I need your advice."

Tom smiled, eased himself into the cushioned metal glider and began to push off slightly, rocking and looking interested, prepared for conversation.

"I feel like I did when I left the Women's Army Air Corps to start teaching in '45. You reminded me how successful I had been training new recruits, assured me I'd be a good teacher."

"You proved to be great with your high school students. Go ahead, take another chance." He nodded encouragement.

"But I'm older, and you're not here."

"Older, wiser, stronger — you love teaching art and you'll be doing that."

"Yes, in many ways, painting will strengthen me. Art. It's such a large subject isn't it? Feelings. Another large subject. And that is all there is. Art for the intellect is better left to the intellectuals; colors, shapes, and the composition of the piece must shout its vibrancy or wake the viewer's soul to the possibilities inherent in a deceptively quiet work."

"See, how passionate and self-assured you are. Be fearless, you don't need me."

Fearless? Since Tom's death, she felt fear and anxiety daily. Ada walked up the concrete steps to stand in the spot where Tom had been. Then she sat on the glider in his empty place. She understood his words intellectually, but couldn't accept the simplicity, or his casual tone. She slipped off her loafers and tucked her feet under one of the cushions at the end of the glider. She let Tom's memory fade, and began to sort through her day without Tom's influence.

CHAPTER ONE

She had been working as a teacher in the inner city high just at the edge of Georgetown proper for the past twenty-five years, since 1949, the year she graduated from George Washington University. She had, with a great amount of reluctance, quit with a plan to open a small business where she could teach art to grown-ups and children, instead of to teenagers. Where her business partner, Jayne, the one with the financial sense, would oversee the administration of the art shop. Jayne envisioned smooth sailing at every turn, but Ada had her doubts although she also felt that this step was the next one and felt clear in her decision to resign her high school teaching position. Still, these last few days at school had been tough.

Earlier that afternoon, she saw Roberto shuffling from the direction of the cafeteria towards her classroom, empty now except for several cardboard boxes of packed art supplies. His head looked too heavy for his neck, not a posture he normally assumed, and Ada wondered what was distressing him.

"*Que pasa*, Roberto," she said a little too loudly for his comfort. He could not escape now. He looked at her tentatively, deciding whether to revert to his machismo persona. He looked at Mrs. Ada Gant, his art teacher, who would be his friend if he could trust for a minute.

Come on baby boy, Ada thought, come on kid, walk into the room. He did. Roberto barely moved his feet, pretended to scrape some dirt off one very expensive, very worn pair of Nike's, and walked into the room with his hands at his sides, flexing first one, then the other, methodically and absently. His face was pale, gray eyes more full of smoke than usual, and not with his sexy, vibrant kind of daredevil smoke. That day it was the smoke that had settled over a burned out city.

He knew that *que pasa* was one of 10 Spanish phrases Ada understood and could speak without embarrassing herself. It was kind of a joke between them. He'd say something like *multo musicale* back, part of a phrase about the Italian language that she taught the art class one day when they all needed a laugh. *Italiano e una bella lingua, multo musicale.*

That day he did not play along and she knew he would not. He looked at her, shook his head, and slouched onto one of the tables just cleaned of acrylics, brushes and water jars, and he said nothing. Ada waited. He looked up at the ceiling, struggling with his jacket zipper trying to pull it open with one hand, failed, looked at it finally to get it right, and ripped it open with both hands to let some breath out.

Again, Ada asked him what was going on.

He asked Ada whether he could borrow some money for cigarettes. He smirked. She looked at him, raised her eyebrows, still waiting.

"No?" he asked, then made as if to get up and leave.

"Roberto, you don't look like a cigarette is what's really on your brain." Ada felt exhausted for this boy, for all the kids in 1974, for their teenage years, for their bumpy emotions, for their shifting landscapes.

He smirked even more, turned his head away, snapped it back to stare at her defiantly.

"How would you know, Mrs. Gant? You don't know, that's how. YOU DON'T KNOW!"

She said nothing, hoping he wouldn't leave if she remained mute. After 25 years of teaching high school, student anger didn't surprise, frighten or annoy Ada. She did not find it amusing and did not join in when some of her colleagues, teachers full of their ersatz wisdom and superiority, laughed at students' behavior while sitting comfortably sipping water or coffee on a stuffed sofa in the teacher's lounge. Patience was a virtue hard learned in her rookie years, making the mistakes green teachers make.

Roberto said, "Okay, all right, no, it's not that ... I mean I know you don't know, how could you and..." He could not continue. He slumped. He let loose a short burst of air.

"Roberto, it's okay," Ada said.

Then he began to talk. Roberto and his girlfriend were pregnant. Ada spent an hour and a half hashing through options with this 18-year-old, her most gifted art student. Were they in l ove? (One had to ask this question of a serious, idealistic 18-year-old boy.) Did he want to marry her? Did she want to marry him? Is adoption an idea they can consider? When were they going to tell their respective parents?

Ada convinced Roberto that he needed to first persuade his girlfriend to talk to an experienced counselor and to make an appointment with a doctor. Ada promised she would keep this confidential and offered to help in any way she could. They set up a time he could call her in two days at her office phone number to further discuss the situation.

Ada wondered why she agreed to help with this problem as she watched him saunter from the room.   She had make her break with teaching high school, had weaned herself from the emotional attachments that had been formed with this last crop of students. Hadn't she? And what did she know about him?

That he always had treated her art supplies with respect, that he skipped lunch periods to work on his paintings, that he haunted museums in his free time. Roberto lived with his mother who worked two jobs and was never home; and with four younger siblings, father absent. Ada had mentored him for the two years he took her classes, encouraged him to dream about a scholarship to   a good art school. And he had won that scholarship to the Rhode Island School of Design. She felt obligated now, to help him   through this crisis; obligated to the commitment she made to herself as a teacher to start these kids thinking about the future, especially the good kids like Roberto.

Previously during that day, Ada had broken up a loud, four-letter-word-calling, spitfire fight between two senior girls who were also good kids. No fisticuffs were involved, so she did not fear a broken earring or a jab from a stray elbow as she got between them. These two, Sandra and Lillian, had been at each other's egos for the entire spring semester. Both carried the word "competitive" tattooed figuratively upon their foreheads; it was due to get loud and ugly, and the high drama greatly pleased the voracious peanut gallery of junior and senior boys who watched.

"Leave my boyfriend alone, you big bitch." Sandra's way with words was enough to goad Lillian into losing her equanimity and shouting back:

"You don't have a boyfriend, slutface, you take on the whole school. How was I to know which guy you have your hands on from moment to moment? Put a collar on them, so the rest of us can tell."

The shouting escalated from there and Ada had stepped between them after one more round of sound to remind them that even on the last day of school, words like "bitch" and "slutface" were unacceptable.

At 2:00PM, Ada's department head stopped by for a "short" chat about her ideas for making the new art teacher's transition as seamless as possible. That lasted 48 minutes and left her with   severe head pain and reinforced the belief that she was doing a wonderfully healthy thing for herself by quitting this career.

It was not a surprise to Ada to find so many fries and greasy food wrappers in her desk drawer as she began to clean out and pack up her 25-years-worth of teaching detritus, which the student helpers would carry out to her car the next day. Today, her last day, she never took even the allotted twenty minutes for lunch because she was packing books into neat cardboard boxes, unpinning   posters from walls, and crisis-counseling students. Twenty minutes for lunch, she thought; that was simply a small symptom of a much larger problem that bred insanity in teachers, students, and administrators; with no down time during the day, Ada could easily understand why hyper kids were half-running the asylum.

Roberto and she finished their heavy conversation at 5:30 PM. So that by the time Ada reached her front porch steps and entered into the conversation with Tom, his mention of her deficient sense of humor was the least important idea on her mind.

It was 1974 and the Watergate scandal was making everyone nervous in DC, creating doubts about the sacred office of the President. Maybe that uneasiness had contributed to the squirrelly behavior of her fighting students, and in a different way to the pregnancy of Roberto's 16-year-old girlfriend.

Sandra and Lillian, each separately repentant, found Ada just before she left her classroom. Lil carried a few things to Ada's Rambler. Sandra pretended to help while keeping close watch on her special guy who was hanging about with his pack of buddies, to see that he did not pay too much attention to Lillian or pay not enough attention to her.

Lillian spoke with Ada while the rest of the kids finally came over to the classroom to help load the last of Ada's art supplies. Lil apologized for her part in the fight and said that she hoped Ada did not think less of her or of her commitment to her artwork. Lillian, Lillian, Ada thought. This girl needs a vacation in the serene quiet of the Smokies, or at a secluded area in the Tetons, maybe Canada would be far enough for her to breathe free; at the very least she could benefit from a thorough night's sleep. Ada had never met her parents, but made a guess that Lillian felt enormous pressure from somewhere to live perfectly.

Sandra, the little snip, Sandra smiled at Ada with all the potent sweetness of her age. She turned on every bulb in her face to light that smile. Ada smiled back and reassured her that her semester art grade still remained an A, no her little hissy fit would not alter her hard fought academic supremacy, she, Sandra, was still the top dog. She bounced away with her pert wave and with her special boyfriend in tow.

The rest of the boys left in their pack, in one of the senior's muscle cars, a dull primered 'Cuda Ada thought it was called. Lil got into her own car, a 10-year-old funny little Nash, and drove away too.

CHAPTER TWO

"Roberto, is 'Angel' your girlfriend's real name, or your nickname for her?"

"It's the only name I know," he said.

This disturbed her. The only name he knew?

"Roberto, " she tried again, do you know her last name?"

"Uh, I think so, it's Chabert, like the sound shaabear, soft sh, soft bear, he explained the pronunciation, like he always did her Spanish.

With this additional bit of information, what should be her next step? Again, what was her role here?

"Pretty name. Let's meet, you and I, say for lunch tomorrow, my treat, to talk again after you speak with Angel. We can meet in the park on Reservoir at about noon; I'll bring sandwiches and soda."

"Sure, any time you're buying, I'm eating. I think I can make it by noon because I don't work until two tomorrow."

"See you then, Roberto. *Vaya con Dios.*

"Hasta."

Ada kept the receiver in her hand, depressed the disconnect button and called Jayne to talk this whole situation over with her.

Jayne Smith, (her real name), shouted "HEY" into Ada's ear as the touchtones began. "I'm calling YOU."

"I was dialing you," Ada responded.

"You must be psychic, honey, but you obviously have forgotten our meeting."

"What meeting?"

"The one we postponed from last week because you had too many projects to grade and just had to get those final marks into the office for your students, remember?"

"Where are we supposed to be meeting?"

"Peacock"

"Right, I do profusely apologize and please forgive the error and timing, and I will run right there to meet you." She laughed, Jayne laughed.

Ada walked. The cafe was near the school and near her home; the café was a place where teachers, students, townspeople, dogs, parrots, all beings converged. A funky place near Wisconsin and Garfield, with a tall thin neon sign out front that stood 10 feet   tall and glowed green and gold at night. Jayne sat, back to the entrance, drinking coffee with four men. Ada knew them all from school and from volunteer work at the free clinic, across the street. They and their wives had lived in the Washington of the '60's and early seventies, in each others' neighborhoods, arguing politics, laughing while sitting at dining room tables, keeping their children away from drafts and all cold things.

Jayne and Ada had been friends for years, took the bloodsister oath at age 9 or 10 when they used their little pocket knives to prick the pad of one finger each, watched fascinated as a small droplet of dark red blood appeared, then ceremoniously touched fingers together to cement the bond. Neither she, nor Ada had a sister; Ada's brother was married and out of the family home by that time. The two, Jayne and Ada, romanticized the freedom of the open air and fresh, unexplored sights and sounds. They had recently decided to form a business partnership and this meeting in their neighborhood café was set to formalize the last details for this new venture, an art store they whimsically named "Art for the Soul".

Ada, the art teacher decided to give classes at the store and buy the supplies. Jayne decided she, with her accounting experience, would handle all financial aspects and detailed administrative tasks.

There they were on that Saturday in June 1974, chasing their four buddies off to find their own table and making the final plans for the shop.

"This is it." Ada said.

"No turning back," she said.

They laughed; Ada shook her head once to clear the air and began studying the written list she had prepared:

       1. No eating fries for breakfast.

       2. Think colors.

       3. Call prospective students.

       4. Interview salespersons.

They hoped that the last item would be simple and pleasant and allotted one week for the interviews after advertising in the Georgetown Gazette and on the bulletin boards of the neighborhood shops. Their hopes did not take into account the time of year, or how attractive their art business would be for the just-graduated-from-college-crowd. They should have put a disclaimer in the ads stating "We do not sell papers, bongs, roach clips, or psychedelic posters."

"Some strange people have called for the sales position and I turned them all down by saying it had been already filled." Jayne frowned.

"I spoke with one or two potentials and set up interviews this week. We'll find someone." Ada sipped her beer and eyed her list. "Oh, yeah, I have five women signed up for one of my art classes— a grandmother of one of my senior girls spread the word. And I am scheduled to visit a few elementary schools this week to speak with the principals about summer art classes for that age group. I'm looking forward to teaching in my own space." She smiled and nudged her friend, "Hey, we're doing fine."

"Not bad, and the capital expenses are covered for now, so that's a very good thing. We still need that perfect salesperson."

On Friday, a friendly, alert and smiling matron who just happened to live around the corner on R Street, knocked on the shop door. Jayne and Ada immediately offered her carte blanch hours, free luncheon sandwich, and weekends off if she would accept the offer and free them from the pseudo hippie hoards who, after 3 days, began pestering them with questions and demands such as:

"When are you going to decide?"

or "Please, I've got this other offer so I've gotta know right now.",

and other such rude statements. The classy lady was named Hope.

Hope, Ada thought, — a good thing to remember. Her husband's face faded in, startled her reverie and then disappeared too quickly for her to see his expression. Damn that little trick while she was working.

Thomas had died just last year in November. She sometimes caught herself still feeling sad, as she did while talking with Hope, but could now focus on her present activity a bit better and relegate her feelings for Tom to a non-active part of her mind when they intruded. She took the new employee's tax forms from Jayne to keep moving, while Jayne escorted Hope to the door.

"Suddenly get a mathematical urge?" Jayne teased.

"No, a flashback from Tom," Ada said smiling.

"Good or bad?"

"Neither."

Jayne looked to see how the feelings played across Ada's face as she spoke, judged them to be satisfactory, and gave a small smile to her good friend for support then quickly raised the volume on the store radio and both turned their attention to other matters.

When Ada and Jayne wrapped up the day at the store, Jayne toting all the ledgers and resumes and file folders she had been sorting in the small office she had carved from the northeast corner of the building, Ada sorting supplies, arranging displays in a colorful and attractive way (orange brush handles next to lemon yellow paint tubes, rainbow–hued posterboards beckoning in the six-foot square beveled glass window area, off-white sheets of canvas floating like giant ribbons behind the entire display) Ada headed to her gray '69 Rambler American, sat for a minute behind the steering wheel, checked the mirrors, turned the key and drove to her brick row house on Tunlaw. She recognized in these careful preparations that she was mimicking Tom's driving habits.

She thought about how Tom found the house 10 years before, when prices bordered on the reasonable. She loved it, and its best feature, that square porch where he often materialized, still invited her home each evening.

As she walked across the porch and unlocked the front door pushing it with her slightly overweight hip, Ada opened a space just enough to finesse her body through without leaving an escape route for her black lab, King. She was thinking about Roberto and his girlfriend. He seemed to feel totally responsible for the pregnancy and naturally very frightened for the future;

how much involvement was wise for her? What level of maturity did his girlfriend have? Did that matter when 16 was never a great age to begin raising a child? I am not a counselor, Ada told herself, I am not a counselor. Leave it to the pros. On the other hand....

King waited, wiggling in moderate anticipation for her signal to go wild, then sensing her heavy mood, jumped only once.

"King, old man, what do I do about an 18-year-old boy and his 16-year-old girl pregnant girlfriend?"

"Woof"

"That's right, King, it's a dilemma and you don't want to get involved. That's a big problem today—people who don't want to get involved."

Ada flashed on Tom's adamant refusal to "own a dog". King moved in right after Tom died, a dog Ada had been tending for years as a sub whenever King's owner left town on vacation. King's owner felt Ada needed King and the black lab agreed, making himself her protector and court jester.

"Tom, you would have loved King... Maybe... Doesn't matter, King's here, you're not." Talking out loud with Tom now felt as natural as breathing.

King barked sharply. Ada turned towards the kitchen and saw Tom stooping down to pet King. He didn't speak; King wriggled and Tom was gone.

Ada picked up the beige wall phone's receiver, but forgot who she intended to call and gently hung it up, shaking her head and mumbling to herself "you've lost it now...."

The phone rang. Ada blinked, answered, and heard Jayne's voice talking to someone else — her son she thought— then Jayne spoke into the phone.

"Hey, want to share a pizza? My son, the oh-so-sophisticated-epicure refuses to eat what I've brought home and

I don't want to waste Giovanni's special. What do you say, game?"

"I can smell the garlic from here and yes, I'll be right over with King. He can eat the leftovers." Ada said. She grabbed King's lead, and headed for Jayne's house a couple of blocks away on Huidekoper Place.

Walking with King through Georgetown's June humidity, past the neat neighborhood row houses, Ada remembered her student days at Visitation, a somber fortress, hidden behind an eight-foot stone gray wall that enclosed it completely. She, one of the few day students among the wealthy boarders, played the good Catholic girl part splendidly throughout her four years there and still did sometimes, especially when teaching her students. Hopefully now that she'd be a businesswoman, that touch of prissiness would die. Its death was long overdue. Ada shuddered when she remembered her first year of teaching.

A teenage girl in her art class had become pregnant. And because this occurred in 1946, the attitudes from the school administrators played out extremely less than empathetic. Ada, as a new teacher, found herself caught in the center of this insignificant maelstrom, while immediately siding with the student, she collapsed under pressure from her uptight, married male principal, and backed off from advocating the student's continued matriculation there. She never fully forgot that incident.

Throughout her years of teaching at that high school, Ada did advocate successfully for her students in many situations: failing grade problems, personality clashes with other teachers, students' demands for more relevant curriculum, and most recently, the rights of students to protest against the Viet Nam War. Was she ready for a teen pregnancy problem?

Jayne and Ada ate the pizza sitting companionably in Jayne's bright, miniscule row-house kitchen and talked about how smart they were to hire Hope, laughed at their complete luck in that matter, and then Ada began speaking about her concern for Roberto and his life's direction.

"Why don't you go with him to talk with the Chabert girl's parents?" Jayne responded.

"Maybe."

King walked her back home. She found two messages taped to her back door, one from Sandra asking for her final grade so that she could tell her parents and get to go to the special-something-or-other-outing which she could not wait to attend; and the other from a woman leaving a phone number, that Ada didn't recognize. It was 10:30PM and she decided to call them both back the next morning.

At 3:30 AM, she was awakened by a vivid dream, somewhat nightmarish, that she couldn't grasp clearly, and she lay in the bed waiting for her mind to put the pieces together.

Thomas. Always it proved to be him still intruding on her space, even if gently, even while she slept. There he sat, at the kitchen table, simply sitting, waiting.

"What on earth?" Ada rustled the pillow and sheets with her arm to dispel the ghost. She wanted sleep, and she began thinking of the two phone calls she needed to return. Then she saw the clock again glowing 3:32 AM— she did not get up.

"I'll be damned, and I won't be, before I lose any sleep over this," she vowed. A few breaths, a few moments of conscious, focussed relaxing of leg and throat muscles, and she fell back to sleep.

At 7:15AM Ada's phone woke her. She felt unreasonably angry. She, who usually felt alert and content upon rising, grabbed the receiver from the black Trimline next to her bed prepared to sear her caller with words of fire at the rude timing of the call.

"Mrs. Gant?" a quiet female voice asked.

Ada's fire banked. "Yes, this is she," she answered letting her tone ask a question.

"Forgive the early call, please, I am due at work in a few minutes and cannot phone from there. I'm Mrs. Chabert and am calling about my daughter, Angel. Do you know where she is?" The woman's tone was so far into frosty that Ada spontaneously shivered.

"Is your daughter Roberto's girlfriend Mrs. Chabert? — so sorry, I'm still waking up."

"Unfortunately, yes, Mrs. Gant." (more frost this time). "Yes, she and that Roberto think they are in love."

"I don't know where she is. I haven't met your daughter Mrs. Chabert, but Roberto has spoken of her with respect…"

"Angel mentioned your name last night and something about talking to a counselor. She's gone, Mrs. Gant. It seems rather suspicious that she'd leave after speaking about your advice. Why would she need to see a counselor? Is that where she is?" Mrs. Chabert demanded, unmelted.

Ada mobilized all her thoughts about Roberto, the pregnancy, (of which Mrs. Chabert seemed unaware), and her own role as a mediator as well as an advocate for youth, who may have no other adult on their side.

"I have to go to work now, Mrs. Gant, and she better be here when I get back or you'll hear about it." The phone slammed from Mrs. Chabert's side.

Ada swore under her breath and began grabbing at her casual clothes, jeans and a loose shirt she kept on a chair near her bed.

"Aggggggh!," she exploded into the air. King ran in with his "what-what?" look prepared to attack, or at least to jump on the bully that seemed to be Ada's enemy.

"Forget it King. There's no one here, just me mouthing off. Just another day at the office. Another parent blaming the teacher. God help us all."

CHAPTER THREE

Lillian ran until her lungs burned. Up those steps from M St. to the top, all those steps that the Georgetown crew members used to bulk up their quads and to increase their wind. This is really hard, she admitted to herself, sweat dripping from her bushy eyebrows, coating her long neck and pooling between the small breasts that she felt embarrassed her mother. She ran north on 36th, past the Tombs bar, past the church, up and around the corner bordering the University she'd be attending in the fall. September was not that far away she reminded herself, keep running. Around that block and north again past Visitation High School, across Reservoir Rd., up north towards her parents' house. She didn't consider it hers anymore. She was a college student now, almost. She ran on Tunlaw and looked up at Mrs. G's porch to see if King would look out the door's side window at her. No, not today. He must be out back in the small yard where he likes to spy on the cat next door.

She laughed at that thought— King spying on the cat— as if he would ever catch it or even eat it if he did catch it. King was a kind-hearted old thing except when someone threatened to step too close to Mrs. G while she walked him. Lillian realized King would bite someone without a second's hesitation if that someone harmed her former art teacher.

Lillian ran all the way west to 40th St. where she slowed her pace, then she walked north towards American University, and eventually to her parents' home. She stretched on the side steps of the old brick house, pulled up one leg to meet her hamstrings, then set it down and pulled up the other. She crossed her legs, standing upright, then she bent over at the waist slowly reaching for the grass near the steps. She did not bounce. Her leg muscles were in top shape and she had no intention of pulling or straining anything this summer. She had a job.

She walked up the four steps into the small enclosed side porch, turned right into the arched kitchen entryway and opened the kitchen door.

At 11:20 or so, she was alone in the house. The younger kids were swimming and both parents at work. The kids were well supervised by the 14-year-old next door who loved making money babysitting and bossing. Her brother and sister didn't take much to bossing, so Lillian laughed at that thought just as she had at the idea of King catching that cat.

Eighteen was a great age, Lillian knew. No more babysitting, no stiff curfews, no high school. Life could not be brighter she thought, and ran up the narrow staircase to the second floor, peeling sweaty tee shirt and bra off as she entered her room. Forty minutes until she needed to leave the house, enough time for a quick shower, lunch and drive to work for the noon to six shift at Roy Rogers on Wisconsin Ave.

Working six hours a day is perfect she felt and she especially liked the busy times when she'd see her friends who'd come to eat a roast beef sandwich or some chicken with those tasty coffee milkshakes (her favorite).

You couldn't find coffee-flavored milkshakes anywhere else, at any other fast food place in the area. That's why she chose to work at Roy's. Anyone can work at Micky D's or Chicken Delight, she thought, but that Roy Rogers was unique and served the best fast food in northwest Washington, D.C.

"May I help you? " Lil asked the next girl in line.

"Oh definitely Miss," Sandra said with a sneer. "I'd like a regular roast beef, no cheese, no sauce, no bun, and pickles on the side."

Perfect, Lillian thought. "Hi Sand," she said.

"Lillian!" Sandra feigned surprise. "I didn't recognize you with the uniform and hat. Stylish."

Lillian ignored the sarcasm, gave Sandra a plate with two slices of roast beef topped with four dill pickle rounds.

"Anything else?" she asked.

Sandra shook her head, took the plate and moved on to the cashier who took one look at the naked food and waved her on without charging a cent.

"That girl needs help," she said over her shoulder to Lil and they both broke out into muffled hoots and suppressed giggles. Lillian checked to see that Sandra had not heard the laughter because she felt almost pity for her prissy nemesis, and there was no need to resort to Sandra's mean-spirited behavior on that perfect summer day anyway.

At six, Lillian left the restaurant, and drove home. Her parent's house was surrounded by four fire trucks and firemen drenching the roof where she could see a small burned-out opening above the back bathroom. The kids and babysitter sat on the lawn, no sign of mother or father.

CHAPTER 4

"Roberto called, Mrs. G, the number's on the pad and I'm off to work. Catch ya later."

Ada marveled at Lillian's energy. She marveled at any energy in any human during these dog August Washington, DC days. She sweated over to the phone and looked at the message written on the pad:

"Call Roberto ASAP!!! 555-2877" written in Lil's giant, hurried script.

All those exclamation marks just killed any little motivation Ada had.

"King, King. Come on boy, I know it's a steam bath out there, kid, but we're going anyway. I need a Coke and you need to pee. Up and at 'em."

Ada finessed King, who's constitution like hers made humid weather a hateful obstacle, all the way to the Georgetown Safeway. She could tie him in the entry there, and he'd be cool while she shopped. She planned to stay at least 20 minutes to enjoy the notoriously frigid air conditioning, chat with a neighbor or two, and gather her wits for the call back to Roberto.

"Good morning Mrs. Gant," a sing-songy voice behind her in the soft drink section called.

She waved backwards without turning, grabbed her six-pack and continued walking. Sandra was not who she needed to chat with then and furthermore she was retired from all obligations to her schoolteacher past. Now she could pick and choose her teenage acquaintances, if any, and leave the irritating kids be. Ada smiled wide at that thought, fairly dancing a small jig smack into Jayne.

"Hey! The heat's really gotten to you babe."

"It's not the heat, it's the motion," Ada replied paraphrasing one of her favorite Maria Muldaur songs.

"Funny." Jayne was not smiling.

"What?" Ada asked.

"Ah nuthin', really, just a small glitch in my accounts."

Ada's eyes widened, she stopped tapping her feet, grabbed Jayne's nearest arm and put the six-pack in Jayne's cart.

"Tell me it's not our accounts. Not the store's accounts, right?"

"Sorry. Yes, it is, but I'm going back this afternoon to double check."

"Shit."

"I'll call you — take that evil caffeine-sugar-empty-calorie soda out of my cart, you dissolute one. Talk to you later. Bye." Jayne zipped away to check out.

Ada wandered into the pasta section, picked up some ziti, some spaghettini and a box of agne di pepe. This should get me through the weekend, she decided, pasta and Coke — it's almost the real thing.

To avoid Sandra in the express lane, Ada waited behind nine people to check out, then remembered King's bone and stepped out of line a second too late. Sandra spotted her again and this time came up to Ada's face making retreat impossible.

"Mrs. G, I've been meaning to call you, I mean Lillian-at-your-house. Isn't it awful about the fire? You were so nice to take her in! What would she have done? I'm sure I don't know what-all I'd do if that happened to me. Isn't it awful, I just..."

Ada cut her off before more drama could ensue.

"Yes, yes, Sandra. Nice of you to think of Lillian. Do call her, dear. Gotta run, bye now, bye."

Ada scurried to the meat department. She really felt bored by that girl's dissembling behavior.

She and King waded through the swamp air back home. This first Saturday in August she should be at the damn beach in Rehobeth, not burning her sandled feet on 36th St. Good idea. No, great. All the beach traffic will be gone (it was 12:30) and we should get there by three at the latest.

"Let's hustle, King, we are out of here."

Leaving a note for Lil with a bag of pasta on the kitchen table, Ada grabbed her swim bag, King's long lead, some of his food, water bowl, the cooler filled with ice and soda, her small portable water color kit, and packed the car trunk. She walked past the phone but deliberately refused to look at the message pad. Deliberately.

"Hey lady, what's that supposed to be?" Four boys under 10 were grouped behind Ada, watching her paint and throwing sticks for King to fetch. It was the smallest boy who was the most inquisitive.

"Do you have art classes at your school, Timmy?" Ada had asked his name when he first ran over to her blanket, ecstatic to find a large friendly canine playmate.

"What's art?" he countered, "like coloring?" His eyes squinting, red buzz cut dripping sweat, he pilfered a handful of her corn chips and sat his sandy body, feet and all, on her blanket.

"You could think of it like that, coloring could be a small part of art. Do you make pictures with your crayons or paint with brushes on a white sheet of paper at school?" Ada willed him to say yes. She didn't want to think about those damn Nixonite Republican school cutbacks in the arts, not on this glorious beach holiday she had carved out for herself. She decided not to let him answer and instead began to explain.

"Art is the name for all things that make you stop and look and wonder. Or you might hear art; because music is art and a poem you read out loud is art and a story your parents read to you is art too. Art makes your heart feel happy or even sad. It can be so mysterious that your mind needs to ask questions just to find out what it is— like this water color picture I'm painting, for instance. You asked me what it's supposed to be, right?"

She let him nod, but before Timmy could open his mouth Ada went on.

"Art is also sculpture, statues you see on the town green here in Rehobeth or Easton. Quilts even, handmade bedspreads with colorful designs like this one we're sitting on can be called art. See the bird pattern here and the star on this side? Art can be something made from materials like cloth or bronze or paint and paper or it can be something that you can't see like a song you hear, like…"

"Like Crosby, Stills and Nash?" he asked.

"Yes, like that, or did you ever hear or sing "America the Beautiful?"

They both began "Oh beautiful, for spacious skies…" They laughed and Ada fell in love with the sparkle in his dark blue eyes. He got it, this kid had an artist's soul. She gave him a high five in delight.

Timmy jumped up and ran to join his three companions who had wandered away when Ada began her monologue.

Hey, Ada mused, one artist out of four is damn good, indeed. Nixon and his policies notwithstanding. Oh shit, she was back thinking about him again and she had pledged to avoid the political sturm and drang this summer. She had gone so far as to cancel her Washington Post subscription. For years all her energy not reserved for her art, her students, or her husband had been sapped by anti-war and anti-administration activities. All that anti-talk, talk, talk. She had retired, damn it, she wanted one summer off from this stuff. She wanted her little art store and time to breathe. Was that so heinous?

Her painting took on a startling, brilliant tone, mostly crimson at the center. She loved it.

Looking out at the ocean, Ada saw Tom standing in the waves, his pants were rolled to the knee and she recognized those skinny legs on that tall body. She began to speak to him about the art lesson she had just given Timmy. Art and love were inseparable for her, they connected to her feelings for Tom.

"I miss having you here Tom. Taking on this new business. You often helped me to take risks, make changes. You told me jokes, chased away some of my fears. And I could have asked you about Roberto. What do I do there? How much responsibility should I assume? "

Tom smiled at her, walked up the beach and sat on her blanket. She could feel his hands rubbing her back, and then a deep warm hug. Ada sat for several minutes feeling stronger and calmer. It was a good day.

CHAPTER 5

"Hi Mrs. G., want some spaghetti?" Lillian garbled, looking up from her plate, mouth stuffed.

"No thanks and why are you eating so late, by the way?"

"We had to work double shifts. Got off at 8. Some kids got fired today for smoking grass on the premises. At least that's what the creepy manager claimed. I don't believe it, he's just prejudiced and those two he fired stood up to him when he tried to make 'em do all the grunt work like closing up three nights in a row. He hates black people and I'll be glad to be out of there when school starts. What's with Roberto?"

"See, that's just the trouble living with another human being—they always catch you slacking off," Ada laughed, but headed directly to the phone before Lillian could utter one word of admonishment. Lillian wagged her finger at her instead.

"I'm calling now, cool it. I needed a mental health day, Lillian, cut me some slack here."

Ada knew Lil would remember this procrastination, this deed not done for a long time. Lil wore her 18-year-old idealism like a party dress. Ada had forgotten so much about being a teenager, how ferocious they could be in any particular situation. No mercy.

"Hello? Roberto? " Ada held her breath, bracing for the emergency he would suck her into. Lillian watched her nod a few times, say "okay, okay", "yes", and finally "I will call you back tomorrow."

"Well?" Lil pounced as soon as the receiver hit the cradle, a big blond insistent catgirl.

"Lillian, sweetie, you know you wouldn't want me to break your confidence, right? You understand. I can't share Roberto's and my private conversations."

"I'll find out anyway, Mrs. G. Everyone talks at Roy Rogers." She picked up her dinner plate and fork, then balanced a jar of grated cheese, a tall glass and two empty soda cans on top and carried it all in her left hand into the kitchen, waving goodbye with her right.

"Goodnight, you perfectly coordinated super-jock-scholar. I'm beat and going to sleep." She heard Lil giggle as she closed her bedroom door.

"Hey Mrs. G, I almost forgot—wow— Jayne called. Said she'd talk to you tomorrow night."

Nuts! Ada had conveniently forgotten Jayne's "small glitch" in the accounts. She thought she might need some wine, or maybe a joint, but with Lil in the house neither one was a great idea. At 18 the kid could legally drink in the District but Ada didn't choose to be drinking buddies with a teenager and couldn't refuse Lillian some if she opened a bottle. She did consider Lillian mature enough to drink, just not tonight, not as a palliative, she was much to young to use alcohol for anything other than youthful celebratory glee. Forget grass— totally, illegally inappropriate. Fanabalah!

Tom's voice glided into Ada's annoyed consciousness so quickly that she snorted. "Fanabalah?" the disembodied voice lilted.

Okay, okay, she thought, maybe not the best mood by which to put herself to sleep. Tom had a habit of making fun of her Italian nonsense words.

"Guess I am waxing dramatic here, Tommy, old boy. What is it that I really want to do? Do I need to get so involved with Roberto and Angel and Mrs. Chabert and that mess? I'd like to offer some support to Roberto, that's clear."

"That's something," Tom responded in his normal, full baritone.

"Oh, so now you're speaking louder. Are you going to appear or do I have the pleasure of your voice only tonight?"

"Voice is quite enough, don't you think?"

"I do, and sometimes that can be far too much for my late-night brain, so perhaps you should let me wrestle with this problem without your input. I do have King, now, see, (King looked up adoringly into Ada's brown eyes) and he doesn't make fun of me with snide "woofs"; he loves me unconditionally."

"Is that what you wanted from me, Sweets? Unconditional love when you admitted that I earned a mere second place in your own affections, second to "your art"—can't have it both ways now, I'm dead."

"Funny. Besides, you did love me unconditionally, you always gave me the bigger slice of cake on my birthday."

"Ada, you did not want me to indulge you. You loved your independence."

"That has nothing to do with King's love for me. He's so cuddly, too."

"Goodnight, Ada." Tom's voice quit.

"King, tonight you can warm up the whole bed while I sit for awhile at my table. That's a good guy." Ada gave the retriever a thorough back scratch and nestled into the fuschia flowered chintz-covered stuffed chair she had placed near the table so that she could comfortably look out the window at the backyard, read, or sketch with all materials close at hand. The nine-foot long tabletop rested upon two sawhorses recently rescued from a protest march along M St., near Key Bridge. She often thought that the large chair and mismatched table suited her incongruous sense of design and color, and gave her unfettered latitude in her work. She needed that sense of comprehensive thinking in order to find a plan, to come to some resolution about her role as Roberto's "helper". She didn't feel very helpful and not a bit inclined to feel more helpful in the days to come—she felt depressed about the teens' sorry situation and angry with herself for volunteering to act as the friend in need. She did not have children for a reason—insanity was inherited from them and after 25 years of dealing with teenagers (the worst kinds of children) she had had enough. Hadn't she?

Ada yawned, stretched and crawled back into bed. "King, move over, and no snoring."

She fell asleep with the somehow cheery thought that her dog didn't move a muscle he didn't absolutely have to move; pure economy of motion.

CHAPTER 6

Ada dialed Roberto's number as she finished the last bite of egg bagel and lox, a taste she had acquired recently from association with the B'nai B'rith ladies who arrived at every Viet Nam protest rally with enough bagels, cream cheese, and lox to feed the idealists.

"Angel and I will get married, Mrs. Gant."

"Roberto, that sounds very nice, and if you have thought about this baby and planned for the expenses and for the childcare while you both complete school, and planned where you will both live, it sounds like you are making a good start."

"Mrs. G, well, we are making a plan. Maybe it's not finished yet, see."

"You mean you have not spoken with Angel about these things, right? Have you talked with your mother?"

"Ai ai ai, non!"

"Why, and please no more Spanish—just some honesty here Roberto. You must begin to take responsibility for your actions. Angel needs to do that as well."

"Mrs. G, you sound like mio madre."

His last sentence gave Ada pause, and she sat at her kitchen table with a cup of coffee to mull that concept over. Roberto's response and his attitude towards her participation didn't convince Ada that he was comfortable with assuming a more mature sense of accountability. She had not foreseen his relegating her to the mother-substitute role when she first volunteered her shoulder to him because his mother, bless her heart-with-all-those-kids, seemed very much the vibrant, strong-minded mama-type. She shuddered.

"Roberto, you two are in big trouble, hot water, *come se dice en Espanol*?

You know this pregnancy is a serious responsibility. WHEN ARE YOU GOING TO SPEAK TO ANGEL'S PARENTS?"

"There's no speaking with them— they yell they give the evil eye, they put on the mean face— they don't talk to me and just about don't talk to Angel neither. I think they want to send her away somewhere."

In the Chabert household, the following conversation took place as Ada and Roberto were speaking:

"Angel is in trouble, Ramon."

"What kind of…you mean…oh shit!"

"Yes, and she thinks she wants to marry the father, some Latino boy named Roberto."

"Shit."

"Is that all you can say? I want her sent somewhere, away from him, have the baby and put it up for adoption. It's the only way."

Roberto's intuition proved infallible. Mrs. Chabert contacted Ada again the following evening by phone to again insist, in her demanding, superior tone that Ada do

something. Do something? Ada thought the woman had taken too many pills, did not utter one word of that idea to her, and said instead,

"I'll be only too glad when this situation is resolved satisfactorily, Mrs. Chabert. Any thing I can do to help you, just let me know."

Mrs. Chabert, Ada heard, choked back a gasp of astonishment at that reply, but gamely countered with:

"Mrs. Gant, I need no help to resolve situations, as you so put it. I am asking you to keep your advocacy to yourself. You know exactly what I mean."

"No, I do not. What are you trying to say, Mrs. Chabert?"

"You, you peaceniks and gay libbers are all the same. You want all the girls to get pregnant and then leave their husbands and love women."

"What?"

"You can't deny it... you are always marching for this or promoting that. Ever since your husband died, your true colors have come out."

"Excuse me, Mrs. Chabert, but are you saying that I am a lesbian?"

"I am not saying anything. Good bye."

Ada sat at her kitchen table stunned and amused at the same moment. Is this what the rumor mill was circulating? She thought she had better check this out with a few of her friends and former students. She also decided to find out a bit more about Mrs. and Mr. Chabert.

"Jayne, hi, what do you know about the Chabert family, Angel's parents? I just received a paranoid call from Mrs. Chabert accusing me of promoting an antiwar and gay and lesbian agenda."

"You must be kidding."

"No, I've just hung up the phone with her and cannot think where she's coming from unless there are rumors floating about. Heard any lately?"

"Not me, but I'll ask my kids and check out the grapevine. Get back to you when I hear something, or not."

Ada called a few more friends, teachers, B'nai B'rith members, and some pals at the Free Clinic. No one knew anything. Puzzling, but not surprising that Mrs. C. might attempt to blacken someone else's name to deflect attention from her own problems at home. Ada put it in that mind compartment and continued her original plan for the day— to paint and paint until the natural light turned and then to get back with Roberto and also with Mrs. Chabert.

"King, what would you say to someone who spread false statements about you?"

The black lab simply turned his back to Ada and walked away.

"I'll take that under advisement."

Ada grabbed a pencil and drew furiously on the reverse of a PEPCO bill. She created a charcoal gargoyle sitting atop an institutional-like building where colonies of small figures appeared to be pouring out of several open doors. A figure was seated inside the building at a desk and Ada knew the gargoyle was waiting to pounce on that one, unsuspecting teacher.

Was the monster Mrs. Chabert? Or some shadow?

She found her 11x14-newsprint pad and several charcoal sticks on a chair in the kitchen and continued this theme on a fresh sheet. A larger, uglier gargoyle took shape, and clamped in its razor-toothed jaw, Ada drew a flailing woman jabbing at the monster's eyeball with a palette knife.

She printed the word "advocacy" on the knife blade and "prejudice" on the flat face of the beast.

Ada sat back in the wooden Eames chair and surveyed her cartoon. Not bad—perhaps The Post would deign to print it. Fat chance with Woodward and Bernstein hogging the headlines in the wilting air of another DC summer. Didn't Nixon resign yet, she thought? How much longer do we here in the US need to put up with Watergate's mess and confusion? Ada stopped her thoughts before she went into before she went into a full rant and began calling all her friends to discuss her displeasure and theirs. The next meeting of her action group was scheduled for Friday; a couple of days would age her thoughts enough to allow her to sound reasonable when she proposed her strategy for the rally next week.

My, she was feeling mature and conservative today! She felt so good that painting a large canvass took up the entire rest of her day, Ada forgot her plan to get back in touch with Roberto, or with Mrs. Chabert. When she remembered these goofs, she did not even blink. "C'est la vie" sailed through her brain as she steeped her best lapsang souchong tea and unrepentedly poured two teaspoons of white refined cane sugar in along with a heavy dollop of cream.

Then Lillian crashed into her perfect kitchen and brought the peace to a halt.

"Mrs. G, what's happening?'

"Not much, dear, it's midnight."

"So?"

"Most adults are winding down now, or sleeping happily in their comfy beds."

"Mrs. G, you have no imagination."

CHAPTER 7

August summer sun in Washington beat upon the heads of all the strollers and wanderers on Wisconsin, near Art for the Soul. Ada and Jayne sipped icy lemonade and marveled at Hope's crisp demeanor, hair perfect, clothes at attention instead of crumpled and soggy, her behavior impeccable.

"Hope, who dresses you in the morning?" Ada couldn't keep her thoughts to herself and her bad humor was beginning to infect her speech.

"Ada, darling, it's nothing. We women of a certain age don't sweat and we definitely do not glow."

Jayne, nearly choking on her drink, chimed in "Ada, and your 100% cotton shirt is simply divine as well, is it new?"

"Funny."

The three of them had been working steadily all day, Hope helping customers, Jayne tracking inventory and Ada in the small art room to the north conducting classes with 9-year-olds who enjoyed shouting out the names of specific colors as they painted their 9x12 posters—alizarin crimson, burnt sienna, flesh (always a favorite), titanium white. Ada loved the energy, but enough was enough. Last class ended at four and the late afternoon wind down with cold drinks and half-hearted complaining became a ritual all three women had adopted.

Hope sat in one of the orange and white striped cushioned rocking chairs the partners placed in a cozy area near the window looking out on P St. She raised her feet to prop them on the matching hassock which also rocked and sipped her still full drink, thoughtfully eyeing the display in front of her. Ada knew she was dying to get her hands on it and change it into a neat symmetrical grouping and wondered how long it would take Hope to make the move. Hope sipped again then put the glass down on the square maple table that stood between the two rockers.

"I think the display needs a little something, don't you, girls?"

Not even two minutes. Ada drank her remaining lemonade in one swallow, shot Jayne a warning look and turned her back to the display, Hope and the front door and pumped her arm in a victory gesture.

"Fine by me, Hope, have at it," Ada said.

Jayne coughed and swallowed, smiled back at Hope and ignored Ada's look as best she could while stifling a laugh and opening up the display door so that Hope could play with the supplies arranged in the window.

Hope methodically moved every piece of the display into rows, the largest sized items in the rear, the smallest to the front. Then she matched everything by color, and finally dusted the entire window almost grabbing the Lemon Pledge until Ada intervened and said

"Hope, honey, please, it's great. The window looks lovely, let's not overkill."

"Oh, Ada, I forgot you're allergic to chemicals. So sorry. No, no chemicals. There. Just perfect."

"Ummhmm," replied Jayne.

"What time is it? Oh, God, after 5, gotta run." Ada sped out the door and managed to round the corner of 35th before letting her laughter out. Several children gave her a wave and laughed along with her for no reason other than that the day was a peach.

Afternoon shadows were just casting shade on the tree-curtained sidewalks of the provincial Georgetown neighborhood and Ada luxuriated in her favorite part of the summer day as she rambled towards 37th St., past the markets near Art for the Soul, and then past stately town houses on R, then Reservoir. She wondered as she walked past their dormitory, what the nursing students at GU for their summer semester thought of the Free Clinic's impending demise. Did they care anymore? It was a very hot project for the kids during the summer of '69 when it opened and she prayed that their enthusiasm still burned, and that the clinic would turn itself around to stick with its original focus and remain free. Another of her pet causes, Tom would say. Tom.

Ada, I see you.

Beautiful day, isn't it?

Lovely.

Ada smiled as she approached her house, talking to Tom silently, wistfully, crying as she opened her front door, softly. King.

"King, don't let the tears upset you, baby, it's all nostalgia, sentiment, you know, poor, poor pitiful me stuff."

"Woof." King sniffed Ada's hand and rubbed his head on her leg, then butted her in the direction of the kitchen and the back door where he wanted to be let out into his backyard paradise. Ada refused to uglify her small greenspace with a fence that would make it seem even tinier, so she needed to watch the dog while he roamed and peed and did his regular business or King would wander off to explore his favorite neighborhood haunts.

"Kingie, good boy, now let's find your leash—go get it, that's it." King raced and almost succeeded in nosing the forest green screen door open before Ada reached it, unlatched it and grabbed the red nylon leash hanging just inside on the wall.

"Let's walk to the park."

Ada and King strolled towards Glover Archibald park, greeting a few neighbors also taking advantage of the cooler evening air. With no warning, Ada's face flushed, sweat poured from her armpits and from under the elastic band of her bra. Puzzled, she urged King into the park and they both jogged up the short rise into the grassy field.

Ada sat on the grass, unhooked King's lead, and swiped at her face which by this time felt flamed by a torch and at the same time weirdly sweaty. She jumped up from the ground and walked quickly towards King, almost running to catch up with the now galloping animal far across the expanse of open greenspace. Big mistake, she thought as she grew dizzy and weaved her way to the dog, looking around to see that no one saw this bizarre, embarrassing behavior. "King," Ada croaked, "come". Of course the dog ignored her completely and ran faster towards the group of trees on the other side of the park, disappearing into the small grove and heading on the path towards the furiously busy Reservoir Road. She was forced to run, breathing like an emphysema patient, avoiding chuckholes and uneven ground to catch him before he made the big break onto the street. "KING, STOP!!" He did turn his head and grin, his tongue-drooping goofily from the corner of his mouth, but didn't slow one bit until he got distracted by the irresistible smell of fresh gore by the side of the path. Ada grabbed his collar as gently as she could while attempting not to collapse in a clammy puddle on the dead squirrel he had discovered.

"Bad dog! You are bad! Heel!" He practically laughed at her histrionics, but attempted to appear chastised and meek for her benefit, hanging his head a trifle and casting his twinkling brown eyes down a degree or two.

Ada wrapped King's lead around a sturdy tree in the shade and sat on the dirt beneath it to catch her breath, and clean her face as best she could with the leafy washcloth she pulled from the branch overhead.

Then she walked with King, now pretending to heel and be led, back through the park, east on W, slowly stepping downhill on 38th and gingerly eased onto Tunlaw until she saw her home. She walked briskly up the gray concrete steps and flopped onto the cushioned porch chair, King lying right beside. As she rested her head against the backrest, Ada felt another wave of fire march up her torso. She sat up, closed her eyes and mouthed "shit". King turned his square head up at her inquiringly.

"Menopause is a bitch, King, be glad you're a guy."

Ada walked into her bedroom and shocked to see Tom sitting on "his" side of the bed taking off his right brogue. The left lay on its side on the floor near his feet. He then peeled down both socks at one time, folded them neatly over his shoes and laid his transparent and fully clothed body on the bed, head cushioned by Ada's favorite pillow.

"What on earth are you doing?" Ada spat.

"Yes, I am on earth, aren't I? Very clever, Ada."

"I didn't intend it to be clever—you frightened me."

"I do apologize, really, I do. Sit. There. See you can sit right on my feet and they won't hurt at all. Now let's speak about this Roberto-lesbian-Mrs. Chabert-accusation-pregnancy-Angel-dilemma."

"All right. Where do I begin? I am angry and disgusted at the behavior of Angel's mother so far in this drama. She seems to be too ready to blame and not at all interested in focussing on Angel's future. The woman has little insight into her own or her daughter's feelings. She seems to be stuffing all the sensitive ones and allowing out only those acceptable to her Puritanical ideals. You know anger, righteousness, scolding behaviors, along with the disdain and blame she uses to punish those who misbehave."

"Take a breath, Ada, you're ranting, I fear."

"You'd better fear, dear...At any who—I seem to be Mrs.C's whipping person at present, along with Roberto (of course the villain), and Angel (led astray by said villain). It seems that Mrs. C has latched on to the far-fetched idea that I am encouraging young teen girls to get pregnant and then ditch their young boyfriends. Thereby a colony of horny young women will form, without men and with babies (not sure quite how this fits her warped scenario yet...), who bond together in a kind of writhing, hormonal lesbos society or something."

"Ridiculous!"

"Yes, isn't it, but sad as well. And I am not about to allow these mean-spirited rumors to prevail, I can tell you that."

"I agree. Shall I give you a weapon to smote the dragons of deceit and treachery?"

"Absolutely, sir Knight."

Tom and Ada spoke for a few minutes more. Ada dropped off to sleep with slightly diabolical grin lighting up her face and King sighed contentedly several times in his dreams too.

CHAPTER 8

Sun lasered onto Ada's mouth and she licked her lips, thinking they were chapped from yesterday's walk and faint in the park, she was still groggy and read the time from her bedside digital watch as 3:14 and couldn't decide whether the streaming light was from a UFO landing or from police swat teams storming the second floor. She closed her eyes again, pulled up the thin flowered Marrimekko print sheet to cover them but couldn't breathe easily and next made the hazy choice of flopping over onto her stomach to continue the night. Darn! Stomach sleeping never worked for her because her neck cricked and pained in so short a time, that she never got the chance to fall asleep that way although the rest of her body snuggled well into the bed in that position. She turned over onto her side, sighed, pried open her eyes with both twisting fists and registered the time as 8:29. Time surely does fly! No, no, she remembered then that she had not fallen back to sleep, must have misread the watch, and woke up completely to the day.

Ada heard Lillian in the bathroom between their two bedrooms, a shower spray, some scrubbing sounds, a whistle that went on for much too long, and then the shower curtain whooshed back on the padded rod. Good, she still had a few minutes to not get out of her antique sleigh bed. Jingle bells, jingle bells. No, stop that, she chided herself, get up, come on old nag, you can do it, up, up.

Quietly, not to alert Lillian, Ada slipped into her flip-flops and glided her feet through her amethyst and peach bedroom doorway, stepped silently past the white bathroom door, stealthily down the narrow 14 oak steps to the landing where she could turn one way to continue four more steps into the tiny kitchen, or the other way four steps down into the sunny living room. She chose the kitchen, in a move as fluid and graceful as her imaginary cat, the one who did not need to be fed, watered or let out.

Ada basked in the sun-warmed kitchen, made a tad too toasty this morning she realized, as she removed the lid from her butter dish and saw the yellow pond floating almost over the lip. Yes, summer in Washington—butter-melting, clothes-wilting, temper-shortening-summer-in-Washington—always predictable.

"It's gonna be a scorcher today they said, Mrs. G."

"Good morning to you too, Lillian."

"What's for breakfast?"

"Pretty funny."

"OK, all right, what do you want for breakfast?"

"Toast, coffee, butter—lots of butter, a new stick's in the compartment in the fridge—and above all, no conversation."

"Grouchy?"

"Zip it."

They ate in silence until the phone rang at 8:36 and Jayne gave Ada the news.

"Sorry, hon, I haven't heard anything useful from my kids. Neither one has picked up any rumors or otherwise (which I guess is a good thing, right?), about Roberto, or about Angel's mother's mental health. Maybe she said those things just to aggravate you."

"Could be."

"So let's not dwell on that crap. Here's something different to think about— I found the problem in our accounts."

"And?"

"Not enough money on the plus side. But I put some in from savings. Not a big deal. You'll see when you get in."

"All right."

"What was that about Mrs. G?"

"Nothing."

"Good, then I have a question about college."

"What?"

"Where did you go to school?"

"George Washington."

"Didn't your husband teach at Georgetown?"

"Yes, he did Lillian, is there a point to this investigation? You know I'm a bear in the morning."

"Forgot. OK. Yes I want to know what to expect when I go to the dorm in September."

"Can we talk about this tonight?"

"OK—I'll stop by Art for the Soul after I get off work at four."

"Wonderful."

"See you then."

Lillian packed all her breakfast paraphernalia in a stack, waltzed it to the sink, ran hot water, let the Ajax liquid drip in, waited for the foam, then shut the tap and left through the kitchen door out onto the alley where she parked her old red Nash in back of Ada's Rambler in the one-car driveway.

Ada could spy on her through the screen door as she sat at the cherry gate-leg table that fit in the kitchen's only open space.

"Amazing, King, that girl has more energy than a superball."

Where is that…just set it down… see the hand placing the glass… where? Ada turned around in a slow circle, scanning her short marble kitchen counter, thought she'd located her juice glass only to be disappointed that it proved to be one of those stupid clear coffee mugs hugging the side of her chrome toaster.

Ada hunted behind the four orange canisters. Of course it wouldn't be *behind;* she grew angry, pushed the wooden cutting board aside, slammed two cupboard doors, then noticed tears from nowhere crawling down her nose and cheeks. She sat. The juice glass sat on the cheery yellow place mat in front of her and Ada stared at it wondering where she could buy a new brain.

Another torrid day and the shop absorbed sun from the arty, but impractical front windows. The A/C – an ancient box unit struggled mightily and stopped at various critical hours— noon, two o'clock when the heat was really broiling, and at 4PM when the heat settled over the city like a wool blanket that wrapped the rush hour in its smoggy shroud. Each time the unit croaked, Jayne tinkered with it as Hope looked on attentively, until it rattled back to life with a geriatric wheeze.

Ada hid in her room which held the "good" air conditioner. She knew that if she ventured through the door into the main store, sweat would pour and embarrass her.

Cooler, better. Hotter, disaster. Mercifully the class consisted of adult women only; kids attended just two days a week, Tuesday and Friday. Those women seemed so relieved to be out of their homes, that they wouldn't blink if Ada stood on her head and spit out wooden nickels, so she felt confident a little hot flash activity, should it appear, would be ignored. Jayne and Hope might make too much of it.

"What color should I make this background sky, Ada Dear? I can't seem to get the proper shade."

"Yellow, light cadmium should work fine."

"Yellow? For sky?"

"What? Oh, I thought you asked me about your subject's uh, shirt, or tie, I think I heard. Did you say sky? How foolish of me, of course sky—you're painting a landscape, anyone can see that." Ada covered awkwardly; her student looked puzzled, but gamely smiled and waited.

"Prussian blue—a little black to darken here and here, and some of this dark purple."

"Yes, thank you, that's what was missing, that touch of black. You are a genius with color, Ada, we are so fortunate to have you giving lessons now to us old biddies, aren't we girls?"

The other three women nodded and clucked and cooed so that Ada felt deeply appreciated and she immediately cried inappropriate torrents, which finally did cause comments.

She laughed them off and her four students left laughing too. Aren't we jolly? Ada thought and kicked her easel a couple of feet for emphasis.

Jayne popped her head in, face puzzled at the clamor, "What's happening in here—I heard a loud noise."

"Nothing."

"Why's your face all red? Are you crying? Ada, what the hell..."

Ada, annoyed and unable to keep up the pretense, began weeping and laughing both, shaking her head vigorously back and forth in denial and slipped on a spot of spilled water from the art class cleanup. She slid into Jayne's backside and both ended up on the linoleum, Ada sprawled over Jaynes's legs, Jayne landing hard on her rear.

"Ow! Damn it! Get off me!"

"Oh God. Forgive me. I'm so sorry Jayne. Are you okay?"

"No! My ass is killing me. Ouch." She stood gingerly rubbing her posterior.

Ada helped her up, brushed off her seat and pant legs and gave her a quick hug.

Hope, who witnessed the grooming behavior after running into Ada's classroom to investigate the second, really loud noise, asked "Were you two fighting in here? Now, what's this all about?"

"Menopause," Jayne blurted.

"Hey!" Ada responded.

"Enough," Hope snapped, "just take it easy, the two of you."

"I am taking it easy, I'm just crying for no reason, that's all, it's not a big deal."

"Until you start whacking the furniture," Jayne countered.

"Oh put a cork in it— wait 'til you start with the hot flashes. I can just hear you moaning and complaining…."

"Me?"

Hope shook her head at them both and walked back to the main store.

"I really don't see why you're carrying on like a 2-year-old, Ada. It can't be that bad." Jayne gave her a disgusted look.

"You have no idea."

"Well, like what? Sweaty face, a few tears— I mean sometimes that happens with PMS and it passes like all things."

"So far it's been several days and the symptoms are NOTHING like any PMS that I've ever had."

"You're just exaggerating, I've seen your sweats and that small heat flush on your face."

Ada realized that Jayne would never have any idea until it happened in her own body and that Jayne wasn't about to offer any empathy.

"Maybe you're right. I'll just go with the flow so to speak."

She finished picking up the art supplies, cleared off the art table, gave Jayne a small smile, and slipped her tote over her shoulder, ready to leave for the day.

Jayne walked into the front room and Ada followed her out, locked the art room, said her goodbye to Hope and walked with Jayne to the sidewalk where they headed home in opposite directions.

CHAPTER 9

A loose-leaf notebook sheet flapped from the refrigerator door in the breeze from the open kitchen window. Lillian's large loopy handwriting could not be ignored, so Ada read it even before grabbing the cut strawberries and heavy cream from inside the fridge.

4:30PM TODAY

Roberto's been arrested. He called here and I answered. Told him you'd go to the jail. He doesn't have a lawyer.

She grimaced as King came up to sniff the berry bowl then haughtily turn up his nose at it. She scratched his ears and poured him some dry food which she'd have to mix with canned Alpo so that His Majesty would eat it. That routine completed, she sat munching on the fruit while contemplating her options. Call Robert's mother? Call a pro bono? Just go to the station?

Ada decided to call the lawyer and drive to the police station. Her work with the B'ni B'rith ladies again provided excellent contacts. Mrs. Adleman knew the perfect lawyer to call, her son-in-law, and gave Ada his phone number.

He answered on the first ring, "Rosen and Rosen," explained the absence of his secretary, "she's on maternity," and agreed to meet Ada and Roberto in 20 minutes at the precinct. Ada wanted to permanently adopt Mrs. Adleman and her earnest son-in-law.

Roberto, sullen and frightened, sat in a straight-backed wooden chair in the station's entryway flanked by one tired, old patrolman and the desk sergeant on the other side.

"This your kid, lady?" the sergeant barked.

"No, but this is his lawyer, Mr. Rosen who has come to get him out of here."

Atty. Rosen and the sergeant spoke briefly, forms were filled out, Roberto released and given no court date, simply a fine of $200. Ada paid it and the attorney left after warning Roberto that a future arrest would likely involve jail.

"What were you thinking? Do you want your baby to have a criminal for a Daddy? What?"

"It was just a little grass, I ain't selling it. I ain't no mafioso."

"Is that supposed to make it all right, that you're not selling this pot to children? I don't think so, Roberto — this behavior shows great disregard for your growing responsibilities. You told me you were making proper plans, consulting with Angel, planning to speak seriously to her parents and your mother. Busted for possession is a poor prelude to the new, responsible you."

"Hey — take it easy Mrs. G. I don't need no lecture."

"You just may — I don't see you acting thankful for your release and I don't hear you apologizing for this stupidity. You're acting like an idiot, and frankly son, I have had enough. Either you quit smoking marijuana, or you cannot be a father. I will oppose your getting any kind of custody of that baby if I find out you're still doing drugs."

"Okay, okay, I'm sorry. Yes, of course I don't want no police record and I don't do drugs. I just happened to have a joint in the car. The cops pulled me over and found it. I didn't even smoke the damn thing. That's the God's honest truth, I swear."

"So why did you have the joint? I don't get it, Roberto. Were you carrying it around for show, to impress your friends?"

"I don't know, maybe, I don't know, some kids were rolling joints, I had to look cool. It's stupid, I know, now it looks so stupid...."

"Roberto, you're smart. Act that way."

"No more drugs. I'll stay away from those guys, I will."

Ada escorted Roberto to the door.

CHAPTER 10

Angel and her mother stood facing each other, Angel a nymph, all dark brown eyes and slender limbs, her mother an older, drier version. Tears sat at the corners of the 15-year-old's eyes while Mrs. Chabert dictated her commands furiously. Angel's father, a bewildered, sad look gracing his features, could only sit at the table between his wife and daughter.

"Mama, you can't do that."

"I can, Angel, you are not an adult, you are living under our roof. We are the parents, not you."

"Papa, Papa, tell her she has no right to take my baby. Roberto and I want to marry. We will take good care of our child. We are not too young!"

Angel's father looked more morose, hanging his graying head for a brief second to compose his thoughts. He slowly straightened his strong neck and faced his wife who's eyes looked blacker, shiny like onyx, and whose beige cheeks had turned to dull crimson.

Mrs. Chabert stared at her husband, never wavering, waiting patiently for him to agree with her, to support the reasonable, easier idea she proposed — adoption for this unplanned baby.

Angel's face froze, allowing her tears to stream from eyes that saw dreams slipping, washing away with each second her father delayed his speech. She would not scream — she was no silly little girl.

Her mother felt Angel's anguish, saw her daughter struggle with the idea that her desires and fantasies were not being supported. Mrs. Chabert didn't intend to cause harsh suffering for her cherished, beautiful girl, but she would not permit her jewel to be stolen from the family by a mistake, an action so thoughtless, so harmful to Angel's happy future.

Mr. Chabert shook his head.

"Angel, I cannot disagree with your Mama. You know she is right, you *are* too young. This is not Arecibo. In the United States the girls go on to college, make a good, smart life."

"I can go to school and take care of my baby, Papa— it's done every day, Madeline in my class has a one-year-old and she's finishing high school, and Cousin Maria — she had a baby at 16 and look — he's a good boy now — no harm has been done, and ..."

Mrs. Chabert cut her off.

"Angel, you are not anyone else. You are our precious daughter. We see what is best for you." She turned from the conversational circle, picked up a dishtowel and began drying a few cups and saucers from the drain board.

Angel slumped into a chair next to her now stone-faced papa. She took the linen breakfast napkin from the pristine white tablecloth and dabbed quickly at one eye, then the other.

"I won't give my baby away. You will see," she vowed in her most refined, adult tone. She finished the now cold buttered toast, drank her orange juice, left the table serenely.

"She's in another world Ramon— she is prolonging this heartbreak."

"Yes, Maria, I see that. She will come around and agree to adoption. Give her some time."

"No, Ramon — no time. She will plan with that Roberto. We must insist that they see each other no more."

"How do we keep them apart? We cannot lock her up."

"We can bring her to stay with my sister in Chicago. Far away. She can stay there with me until she has the baby."

"I won't go." Angel rushed through the kitchen and out the door before her parents could think to stop her.

CHAPTER 11

Ada sobbed when her Howdy Doody souvenir juice glass shattered in the sink. She could not find anything amusing in the fact that she had been much too old for the Peanut Gallery in the show's heyday, and could not possibly have warm memories of childhood attached to the ridiculous glass. She picked at the pieces with a damp paper towel, wanting Tom.

Nothing in her life or in the lives of her friends interested Ada —not even Nixon's resignation at the beginning of August lifted her spirits. She had not heard from Roberto since his marijuana bust. He was to contact her and she did not have energy to call him.

She worked at the store giving lessons, but created no new art for herself. At home she spoke in monosyllables which Lillian tolerated because the girl was too busy with work and school preparation to feel slighted. King coped badly and displayed his betrayed feelings by moping and eating little. Ada resented the extra effort required to entice him (hamburger, hotdogs) when he refused to leave his prone position under the kitchen table for his bowl. She mourned Tom's death deeper than she had during her first few months of widowhood. Yes, she heard that would happen. No, she was not prepared.

When suicidal thoughts emerged after a night's heavy, dreamless sleep, Ada considered various methods and decided they all required too much vitality. She didn't want to die; she simply didn't want Tom to be dead.

Several nights later Ada tossed in and out of slumber, dreams piecing together the darkness, small lights peeping through bedroom curtains. "... November rally..." "Nixon resigned." Loud thoughts both irritating and confusing. Her thoughts, not Tom's voice. She blocked her ears, hummed, swore, lay down as flat as possible without the pillow, breathed slowly, but the same words continued and she was forced to pay attention. She remembered a November peace march, gripping Tom's arm while they ran from tear gas, their discouragement after years of working together to effect change in Nixon's Vietnam policies. Nixon had resigned. Tom should be pleased. Ada fell back to sleep remembering Tom pacing as he spoke to his political science class, those steady, persistent steps matching his lecture's rhythm.

When she awoke at 5:30, she felt a lighter energy within, her legs and arms stronger, eyes rested. Did she feel good? Ada hesitated at good, but she allowed herself to hope she might be feeling less depressed.

King made a noise that sounded close to his normal morning greeting and padded slowly into her bedroom to see why she was awake so early. Ada noted his movement out of the kitchen and at his show of interest.

"King, feeling peppy again?" She rubbed his neck and looked him over seeing that he had lost some weight; she had gained eight pounds. Then, thinking about her "undisciplined" and "bad" habits, Ada lost enthusiasm for leaving the bed. She fell asleep and awakened at two, limbs more leaden than before she experienced the slight revival.

"What now?" She wanted the energy back, craved it, and blamed her physiology for failing her and blamed Tom for dying. Her anger surprised her, pleased her, got her up, dressed and to the kitchen where she brewed a pot of French Roast and fed King. She sat square to the table, spine at full attention while drinking one cup black, then another with sugar and cream. Her dog sat by her chair with his head up, eyes front.

"King, I did not retire from the military to become insipid. Let's move out!" She grabbed his lead, clipped him to it and marched out the kitchen door determined to walk for an hour.

She steered King away from the park, so recently the scene of her embarrassing meltdown, and walked north towards American University. The narrow Georgetown streets flowed into the wide river of New Mexico Avenue and brought them to the Tudor suburb-within-the-city that surrounded AU.

"Let's walk past Lillian's house, King. Check on the reconstruction." A bright blue tarp covered the small roof over Lil's hideaway bedroom, but the rest of the modest half-timbered home looked fine, completely repainted where fire had scorched the second story exterior. Ada shrugged. "Ah, King, we'll have her teen-aged exuberance with us until school starts. Now I get it — that motherly sigh of relief every September..."

They turned near Nebraska Circle and looped home along the shadiest streets, King drinking water from a car wash run-off and stepping through one high-arching lawn sprinkler along the way. Both collapsed at the front porch, Ada onto the glider, where she swooshed back and forth to generate breeze, while King hugged the floor, limbs splayed.

"Ada, it's been longer than an hour. Quite a walk."

"Ha. Where have you been, dammit?"

"Don't give yourself a hard time, baby, that's all."

"You sound like the Magic Eight Ball, Tom."

CHAPTER 12

Mrs. Chabert began the same August morning smiling at her husband over breakfast eggs, sausage and toast. He nodded for the salt and when the air conditioning cycled on, he asked his wife whether she enjoyed that noise better than the sound of Angel's voice. She steeled herself against the bitter remark. "Ramon, you agreed to send her there too. She'll calm down in the hospital."

Her husband said nothing, feeling ashamed that he had signed commitment papers, sending his sweet daughter to a psychiatric hospital. Carson Psychiatric Treatment Center it was called. The building looked like an elementary school, one story of yellow brick in an L-shaped design, just off MacArthur Boulevard in the northwest part of the city. For teenagers with problems. Who doesn't have problems, he thought, do we lock everyone up?

"She was out of control Ramon, threatening to run away if we sent her to my sister's home. Crying, arguing, making no sense. Keeping the baby...marrying — these were irrational ideas. It's just for two weeks."

Mrs. Chabert believed in doctors and hospitals because they kept the world more orderly by removing sickness from bodies and minds and by providing designated places for rest and recovery. Her Angel needed only to be restored to order. The girl had refused to consider an abortion, a quick treatment from doctors and hospitals, and her father had supported that decision. Idealists. Mrs. Chabert looked at her husband and his half-eaten meal, resolving to cook him his favorites for dinner, maybe let him eat in front of the television.

She cleared the plates, put them in the dishwasher and wiped the table, keeping her normal routine, then ushered her husband out the door to work. Her plan to avoid any more discussion about Angel was successful.

CHAPTER 13

Until Lillian discovered through her grapevine that Angel had been sent to Carson, Ada had hoped that the girl, Roberto, and their families had come to a satisfactory compromise regarding the pregnancy. Ada's mood had leveled during the past week, and she had been enjoying small successes at the store — a few more art students and steady increases in sales. Both She and King had settled back into regular eating habits, and life had again appeared tolerable.

"Carson? Has Roberto called me lately? Did I miss one of your messages, Lil?" Ada ate one of Lil's fries, then another; she needed something sweet next and rummaged through the kitchen cabinets until she found a package of chocolate chips.

"No, and I was wondering when you'd talk to him." Lillian put down her hamburger and stared, challenging Ada to take some action.

"Don't you have to work the afternoon shift? It's almost two."

"Not this Saturday, Mrs. G. Want me to call him?"

"That would be interference Lillian, just like in a ball game. He'll call me if he needs to talk, please do not pressure me."

Lillian raised her eyebrows, but finished her lunch talking with Ada only about how quickly the summer had gone. She ran off to visit friends in Bethesda.

Ada called for King. She felt overwhelmed and anxious, sure signs of the necessity for her regular long walk. At least she hadn't eaten many chocolate chips, and for that she patted herself on the back, but still worried that her fresh equilibrium had been so easily upset.

When she returned home, she phoned Jayne to talk about Angel's new situation and received the anticipated rational advice: "This is much too strange for you to be involved with right now. You have your own problems. Take care of yourself."

CHAPTER 14

Angel sat half asleep curled against one end of a beige vinyl sofa talking with Roberto in the dreary smoke-filled patient lounge. He stood at her back, rubbing her shoulders, leaning his head to her ear, while he watched the room. It was filled with several dull-faced or angry teenagers and their anxious visitors, all smoking; two male counselors joking with each other; one girl crying alone, staring at the wall-mounted television set tuned to "The Brady Bunch"; another girl rocking slowly in a molded plastic chair; a few young men playing cards.

"We got to get you out, now — it's killing in here."

"No, it's not, Roberto, I'm all right. See, the baby is growing good." Angel took his hand and placed it on her slightly rounded belly. "I'm eating all the right foods and I don't stay in the smoky places... very much."

"Angel, look around, you don't belong in here." He closed his eyes against the harsh fluorescent lighting.

"So. What do you expect me to do, jump from the roof? 'Berto, be sensible, I'll be home soon."

Roberto knew that it wouldn't get any better once she was back home, but he didn't say that to her. What could he say? What would be best for everyone?

"See you tomorrow, Bonita, sleep well."

He couldn't sleep. His kid brothers and sisters had fought over every aspect of their nighttime routine, finally postponing their bedtime until eleven when their mother returned home from her second job. Roberto had just managed not to slap them all. Then his mother unloaded her day on him. "Si, Mama, that's too much. No, not all the inventory...uh huh, ... uh huh...." By the time she felt good, he felt wired. 2 A.M. 3:24. 4:18. Still awake. He couldn't call anyone at that time of the morning.

Roberto left the apartment to walk to the all night People's Drug store for a bottle of aspirin. His head was pounding. Sticky heat everywhere. August in the District.

CHAPTER 15

Lillian's summer had gone well. Her parents did not phone her much after her first week at Ada's, and when they did call they didn't keep suggesting she return home and sleep on the couch until her room was repaired. They asked her to baby-sit her younger sisters a few times, then found an older neighbor woman to take over that job when Lil needed to take the night shift at Roy Rogers. Lillian was Cinderella no more.

"Mrs. G, let's eat at the '89 — I have to start preparing for my freshman year, you know, hanging out at the 'Tombs' with the rest of the Georgetown undergrads."

Ada appreciated Lil's sense of humor and felt vindicated that her original decision (Lil's boarding with her for a few weeks) proved sound and fortuitous both. Lillian answered phones, washed dishes, cleaned up after herself and walked with King. The perfect house guest.

"When are you leaving to move into the dorm, kid? Not that I'm tired of you ... yet." Ada winked at her.

"How could you ever get tired of me?" Lil put her hands over her heart and smiled angelically. "We have to move into St. Mary's Residence Hall on September fourth."

"All right then, let's see if the old '1789' still serves the best burgers in town and the coldest draughts. Yes, you will need to practice your libation skills to keep pace with those *Hoyas*, but tonight, just one beer with dinner. You're legal, but not by much."

"Ada, what are Roberto and Angel going to do? Can they ...."

"You know, Lillian, I'd rather not think about them tonight, let's enjoy the walk and the good food."

But when they passed Tehan's grocery, a block from the pub, they bumped into Roberto who was walking out of the store at the end of his shift. Ada had forgotten that he worked there stocking shelves and unloading produce.

"Hey, come on and eat a burger with us at the 'Tombs', my treat," Lil said. Ada just smiled. That girl....

"Sounds good." Roberto and Lil exchanged small talk about their summer jobs, while Ada listened, hoping to get through the meal before being required to tackle Roberto's heavy issues.

The three spent a long time eating. First the onion rings, then the burgers, a beer each, another burger for Roberto, more onion rings to split, coffee. Two hours and the "Chimes", Georgtown's elite men's glee club that usually performed at the underground room, did not sing one note. Lillian felt disappointed to have missed them. Ada and Roberto did not.

"You know, I'd like to marry her, Mrs. Gant, and take care of her and the baby when it comes. She thinks everything will be roses and candy when she gets back home from Carson — they put her there for two weeks, a place for parents to get rid of their kids..."

"Yes, Lillian told me she was there," Ada said.

"...anyway, that mother of hers is evil and you know it as well as me. When she gets back home, another brick will fall on her head and then what? It's not right."

"I agree, the whole thing stinks," Lillian said and smacked the thick wooden table.
Mugs rattled.

"Lil, drama won't be helpful, here." Ada turned to Roberto, "I agree with you, that committing Angel to Carson seems extreme. Was she hallucinating or threatening to kill herself?"

"No. She disagreed with that witch, that's all."

"Must have been some disagreement," Lil piped in again. Ada scowled at her.

"Roberto, have you spoken with Angel's parents at all? And what does your mother think of this whole thing?" Ada was relieved that he had not called her during the past few weeks with this new twist to the pregnancy saga, but felt guilty in some way as well. She couldn't pinpoint it.

"I love her, Mrs. Gant. We deserve to have a chance to make a life together. If it's hard, then we will deal with that. Angel will finish high school and go on to college if she wants. I'm still planning to take that scholarship to RISD. I'm packed, and all I need is Angel with me." His voice was calm, his eyes clear.

"She's still a minor, what about her parents' consent?" Ada asked the question knowing he had an answer prepared, wanting to hear it.

"We go to court and get her emancipated. I spoke to some people at the Free Clinic who gave me a number for a lawyer who does this kind of stuff. I read about it too. The lawyer will do it *pro bono,* she said."

Because he spoke so confidently, Ada entertained the idea, appreciating Roberto's efforts to solve his own problem. His reasoning could not be faulted; Angel and he could successfully make a life for themselves with an enormous amount of sacrifice and hard work.

"Anything in this world is possible, Roberto. It all depends on whether one is willing to live with the consequences of one's actions after making a choice. In this instance, Angel, a minor, has more to contend with than do you. Your mother obviously treats you as an adult. Angel's parents treat her as their precious baby. You can't discount that. You will have to live a long life dealing with her family." Ada heard the first four notes of the theme to Zefferrelli's *Romeo and Juliet* play in her head. Then heard "…It's still the same old story, the fight for love and glory, a case of do or die. The world will always welcome lovers, as time goes by." Not always, she thought.

CHAPTER 16

Tom had left Ada a legacy, not much of a monetary inheritance, but a high standard of competency and risk-taking that she had incorporated into her life while they were married, and that she strove to maintain in his absence. When he taught students at George Washington and at Georgetown Universities he searched for creative methods to interest his political science students, making himself available for conferences and after-hours mentoring if asked.

He encouraged Ada to begin teaching immediately after she left the Army Air Corps. "He, or in this case, she, who hesitates is lost," he told her. Tom initiated their involvement with the Free Clinic on Wisconsin Avenue in 1967 and he jumped first on the anti-Vietnam bandwagon. Ada would have let others attend those early rallies and marches in 1969. She would have joined in later, and not have been so fearless without Tom's enthusiasm for the good fight, and his belief that only an activist lifestyle would preserve a democratic nation.

Ada's time in the military had conditioned her to reserve action until extensive planning had lowered the risk of failure, and during the life and struggles of World War II she was well served by conservative thinking. In the 1960's she understood that she needed to "change with the times" as her high school students often proclaimed, and she had modified many of her old attitudes and updated her classroom techniques.

Her artwork changed too, slowly developing an edge, with an innovative compositional structure and a more colorful palate. She experimented with mixed media, using watercolor as a wash over a heavily textured acrylic foundation on some pieces, adding fabric and found objects to others. She urged her art students to paint larger or with twigs, or to draw with the non-dominant hand if they so chose. Ada's political activism and her *avant garde* artistic vision grew directly from Tom's encouragement.

Even with all this history and evolution towards a more proactive lifestyle, Ada was unwilling to act with the same risk-taking abandon with which Roberto seemed so comfortable. She hadn't offered to help him with Angel's emancipation proceedings.

CHAPTER 17

"Mama, take these clothes, please and I'll carry the suitcases ," Angel said. She walked into the shared bathroom between the two four-bed hospital rooms to check on any stray cosmetics. Her three roommates all sat on their respective beds staring at Mrs. Chabert, and alternately chewing red nail polish from their fingers, eating packaged cheese and peanut butter-filled orange crackers. Not one of them spoke.

"Good-bye and good luck everybody. Diana, I know you'll work everything out. You too Sara and Karen. I love you all, thanks so much for everything. I'll miss you." Angel hugged each one and whispered something to Diana, a too thin, pretty girl wearing a bulky navy sweater over a denim workshirt covering a heavy gray thermal shirt with long-sleeves that fell below her wrists. Then she turned to her mother, "I've got everything, it looks like, but I need to say goodbye to the nurses and the counselors. You can wait here, or come with me, OK?"

Mrs. Chabert could not leave the room quickly enough and followed Angel to the nurse's station next to the elevators.

Angel made her goodbyes short except for the long hug she gave one young male nurse named Steve, then she and her mother walked down the stairway exit to the parking lot.

On the way home, driving solely on K, the fastest east-west street in the city, neither spoke. When Mrs. Chabert parked her brown and white Chrysler station wagon in the garage next to her husband's tan Rabbit, she turned to her daughter, "Angel, now that you're home, I think we must make plans to make sure you and the baby are healthy until she is born. What have you been eating in the hospital?"

"Oh, Mama. All the food there was so awful and greasy. Could you please make me some... Oh, I don't know..."

"Angel, what do you want?"

"I want to keep this baby, that's what I want. The same thing I wanted before. Nothing at all is different."

"Let's talk about this after lunch."

"No, I want to talk now. You still don't understand do you? Roberto and I are planning to marry as soon as we can. We are both old enough." Angel spoke in her most reasonable tone of voice but stood with her hands on both hips, and did not smile at her mother. Instead she began clicking her teeth and snapping her fingers to a tune she hummed that sounded to her mother like a big band swing tune from the 1940's.

"I still want to keep our baby...."

Mrs. Chabert could not believe her daughter could be still stubborn after counseling and after two weeks' time to think through her situation. She looked at Angel, her beautiful daughter, and sighed. Angel sat and ate the lunch her mother prepared for her.

Mr. Chabert was not due home until 6 or so, but he left his office early on that day; he worried about his daughter's homecoming.

"Angel, you're home." He gave her a big smile and a quick hug, then he held her at arm's length and shook his head. "So thin, my baby girl, didn't you eat at all?"

"Oh Papa — of course I ate. The food was too greasy, that's all. I ate, don't worry. See— I'm not so thin." She put his hand on her small protruding belly. "The baby is fine."

"The baby. Yes, I can see the baby is growing, but your face is so drawn...."

"Stop it. I am fine."

""If you say so." He would not let it go, and his tone held the same old question
Angel had heard all her life. He really was so infuriating. Couldn't he be on her side for once, she thought?

Mr. Chabert looked at his wife. "She looks all right, then?"

She gave him an impatient glance.

Angel turned to her mother. "Mama, you know I'm eating healthy, right?"

Mrs. Chabert didn't say a word. She looked at her daughter directly in the eye and said, "Are you done here?"

The white kitchen wall phone rang and Angel walked between her two parents and easily reached for the headset, put it to her right ear listening to the silence for a short while before she said "Hello" in an even tone of voice. She heard Roberto breathe a quick sigh and then heard his voice. "Hello, so you made it back home."

"Yes, as you can hear I am here. How are you?

"Good. Very good here."

"Yes, everything is fine here, too."

CHAPTER 18

Ada and Jayne worked a 10-hour day on September 4th, the hottest day of the summer. "Art for the Soul" had been busy because colleges were soon to re-open for the fall semester and students needed to buy art supplies for all their classes. Just one month previously Richard Nixon had resigned after months of hounding from Bernstein, Woodward, *The Washington Post,* and most all the citizens of the nation. Watergate had been a running sore point for the country since the 1972 elections. A break-in at the fan-shaped Watergate office building and apartment complex during the hotly contested U.S. Presidential race of that year, brought the nation to its knees as Halderman and Erlichman advised Mr. Nixon and Spiro Agnew abused his wife. All the abuses that existed during Nixon's Administration were uncovered for the entire world to read. Interestingly, Mr. Nixon was always revered overseas in countries like France and China where he took the advice of one of his advisors, Mr. Henry Kissinger, and attempted to normalize relations with that Communist country. Mr. Nixon was not revered in the United States after the scandal was exposed and he wisely resigned his post as President of the United States.

It was a tearful goodbye on the south lawn of the White House grounds, family at his side, both arms extended upward as he walked smiling through his tears to the awaiting helicopter.

Ada and Jayne sat in their office talking about the kindness of Jerry Ford. He took over the Presidency as soon as Nixon resigned. One of his first acts as President was to pardon Richard Nixon. He said nothing to the press about why, or anything else that was asked of him regarding that decision. The country took a breather, and Ada, Jayne, all their friends and almost everyone else in the Washington, DC area felt the pressure lift.

"It looks like the store is going to make a profit by the year's end. What do you think?" Ada asked.

"I haven't accounted for last month's receipt's nor this month's yet, of course, but by the first of October, I should be able to estimate how far we've left to go. Six months is not a very long time to start seeing black ink. We were not under capitalized, but we're not rolling in it, and those bank loans still need to be paid. I'd guess if I had to, that by next March, it could happen, maybe sooner."

Ada looked at her business partner and shrugged. She didn't really concern herself with a time schedule, she focussed only on the progress her students were making and on her own art work. That was enough for her life at that moment.

Hope knocked on the office door, and peeked her head in.

"I'm going home. Be sure to lock the double doors in the alley when you finish the books, girls."

"We always lock the doors, Hope." Jayne said.

"Not last night. I found them unlocked this morning when I opened." Hope shook her head and then said, "I forgot to tell you that Lillian called earlier this afternoon for Ada. She picked up a message someone left on your front porch, Dear, taped to your glider. Least that's what she said to me."

"What message? From whom?"

"She didn't tell me who left it and she asked that you not stay at work too late tonight. Something about an appointment or a meeting...." Hope smiled and shut the office door, and walked away towards the front of the store.

"How many students have you taught since July 1st? Do you remember?" Jayne asked.

Ada looked through the small window that separated the double office from her art room. She counted the standing easels she could see and estimated that she had set up four more around the perimeter near the walls where the shiest students attempted to hide during her classes. "I'd guess about

16 from July first until today. I expect more students to sign up after the area colleges begin the semester on September 15th."

"You are the eternal optimist." Jayne laughed.

"Why not?" Ada quirked one eyebrow.

"Suit yourself, that's what I say." Jayne quirked one back at her.

Ada straightened the few papers on her desk and put her sunglasses on. "I'm out of here. Bye." She walked to the front of the store and exited through the P street door, heading towards Wisconsin. She wanted to walk home past The Peacock to check whether her group was eating supper before their regular seven o'clock meeting. She strolled up to the tall glass window in front of the neighborhood restaurant and looked in. She saw a few friends, but not the small circle she was to meet later, so she continued north on Wisconsin, cut over Calvert onto Tunlaw and to her home. Then she remembered the note Lillian called about earlier. She supposed that Lil left it for her on the refrigerator door.

Ada sat on her porch for a few moments, enjoying her solitude. She felt that the day had gone well because a few more art students had called to inquire about future classes in drawing as well as about her ongoing studio classes in oil. She pictured her newest canvas that sat upstairs in her personal space, on the easel she'd received as a tenth anniversary gift from Tom. She began to compose the landscape of the eastern Maryland shore in her mind's eye. Her preliminary sketches were good, but something still   did not quite suit her aesthetic sense. She'd have to ponder it a few more days. Ada relaxed into the warm September air and closed her eyes for a short time.

CHAPTER 19

Lillian felt excited. She packed her fall clothes and some lighter, summer blouses too. She looked forward to the start of classes. She had been reading books on government during the summer, and talked with Ada's small group of activist political friends on a couple of occasions when they met at "The Peacock.'

Lil was excited to be attending the Georgetown School of Foreign Service because her dream was to become a counsel at an American Embassy somewhere in South America. She spoke some Spanish, but Portuguese seemed trickier to her and she'd be taking Portuguese in language lab second semester and all during her sophomore and junior years.

She and Roberto had become Spanish-speaking buddies during the last few weeks of summer. Both had been in Ada's art classes their last two years at high school, but both of them had worked after school and had no real chance to become friends at school.

Lillian had spoken with Angel over the phone a few times during the summer as well. She knew from her experience taking care of her younger brothers and sisters that Angel would need a young woman's perspective and shoulder to lean on; talking on the phone seemed to be Lillian's forte`.

Ada walked into Lil's room to check on the packing process. All seemed in order and Lillian was not rushing or throwing items into her suitcases like a crazed banshee. Ada smiled. The chick was leaving the borrowed nest and with strength.

"Are you allowed to keep your car on campus these days?"

"Mrs. G, are you still living in the dark ages? Of course — but we need to register it and get a little sticker."

"Good for you because I didn't want to deny a request from you to park it in the back alley. By winter, some snow or ice would be nuisance with two vehicles there."

"And I wouldn't leave it with the parents. Who knows who'd be driving it then."

"Lillian, surely they have their own cars."

"You never know."

Lillian and Ada carried the suitcases to the little Nash and locked the trunk.

"You don't need me to help you move into the dorm, do you? I know you've visited twice already and have your room and roommate all set."

"Mrs. G — its six blocks away! It's not as if I'm moving to Kansa, Utah or someplace. Don't worry, I've got it all under control."

"Lillian, you've got a lot to learn."

Ada smiled and gave Lil a hug. Lillian tooted her horn as she drove southeast on Tunlaw towards the University. Then she stopped her car and backed up quickly, leaned out towards Ada, "Let me know what happens."

'With what?"

Lillian spoke to Ada as if talking with a child, "Remember the note Roberto left you?"

Ada's mouth dropped. "I didn't read it yet. Assumed that note was from one of my Peacock friends about our meeting tonight."

"Nope. He wants you to meet him tonight, 7:30 at the Peacock. I told him you had a meeting there at eight." Lillian drove away.

CHAPTER 20

"King, I had hoped Roberto would work through Angel's emancipation scheme without me. He has a lawyer, why do we need to meet? You're coming with, I need your support."

Ada and King walked the few blocks to the restaurant, Ada muttering to the dog and he, listening and trotting ahead. Roberto stood waiting by the side of the tall wooden door, his face shaded green by the neon "Peacock" sign. He motioned to Ada and turned towards the four-car parking lot.

Angel sat in his dark blue Fairlane watching the three approach as she munched daintily on a piece of fried chicken. King ran to her open window sniffing hopefully and Angel gave him half of her snack. "Such a beautiful dog." King grinned at her.

"Mrs. Gant, this is Angel Chabert. Angel, meet Mrs. Gant." Roberto spoke softly, unsmiling.

"I have heard so many good things from 'Berto about you Mrs. Gant, it's nice to meet you at last."

"It's good to meet you too, Angel." Ada took the girl's hand in both of hers and held it for a few seconds.

"Let go of her!" Mrs. Chabert marched to Ada's side and grabbed her daughter's hand from Ada's clasp. Angel pulled her hand away from her mother and quickly rolled up her window and locked the car doors; King growled and stood between the car and Mrs. Chabert.

"King sit!" Reluctantly the dog obeyed and, Ada snapped the lead to his collar wedging herself between the two adversaries. "He won't hurt you, Mrs. Chabert, as long as you don't grab me again."

"I didn't touch you— I merely took my daughter's hand. Don't threaten me." She glowered at Ada.

"Mrs. Chabert, it's all right. Calm down." Roberto moved towards the two women, both of whom scowled at him.

"Roberto, we are quite calm and capable of monitoring our own behavior. Isn't that right, Mrs. Chabert?" Ada successfully drew a curt nod from the other woman and Roberto backed away saying "Sorry".

Ada looked at Angel, aloof, locked in the car pretending that no one could see her, and at her mother, furious, pretending that she was in control. This was no courtroom, no decorous emancipation hearing. No, this was the down and dirty parking lot at the "Peacock", of all places. She heard the overture from "West Side Story" steal into her ear and she coughed to buy time.

"Mrs. Gant, what are you doing here with my daughter?"

A fair question, and one for which Ada needed a brilliant answer. "I don't know," is what she replied instead. "Roberto, can you help us out here?"

He explained to Mrs. Chabert that he had called Ada.

"But your note mentioned nothing about meeting Angel," Ada said to cover her derriere. She affected an exaggerated quizzical expression to add to her credibility, but Mrs. Chabert did not seem impressed.

"I drove up to my home, to find my daughter in your car, Roberto, and you driving away. Naturally I followed you to prevent Angel from doing anything foolish. And what do I see? My daughter is in a parking lot at a bar. And Mrs. Gant, you think this is proper?"

King looked at Mrs. Chabert then at Ada. He decided to let Ada handle it, and lay down, eyes closed.

"Mrs. Chabert, I've found in my experience teaching, that often we adults must talk with teenagers when they are available, wherever they are. Please, let's not lose this opportunity. Roberto, please ask Angel to come out of the car and join the conversation."

She heard Tom whisper "Good move, Ada."

"As if I didn't know," she whispered back. King smiled.

"Angel, come with me. Now!" Mrs. Chabert glared at her daughter as Angel opened the door. Angel stepped out of the car and went to stand near Roberto. Her mother stamped her foot, and advanced towards the two teenagers.

"She is going to be my wife. You must see that it's what she wants. You cannot force her to give our child away." Roberto had raised his voice to match Mrs. Chabert's tone.

Ada decided to keep silent and let the anger fly. These three needed to face each other.

"Is that what you want, Angel, to marry this boy? How can you think such a marriage will work? "

"Mama, let's talk about it, not shout. Can we do that? Can we go talk with Daddy, now?" Angel squeezed her mother's arm. "Please."

"I don't see what that will solve." Mrs. Chabert lowered her voice, shook her head.

"Mrs. Chabert, at least give us a chance." Roberto softened his tone. "We will follow you to your house."

"I must be crazy to say yes, but all right, come. We will talk about this, but I am not promising anything." Mrs. Chabert got into her car, waited for Angel and Roberto to get into his, then led the way out of the parking lot.

EPILOGUE

Ada returned from the "Peacock" too energized to sleep, so she decided to finish writing checks for her PEPCO and AT&T bills. King walked upstairs with her but turned into the bathroom to lounge on the cool floor tiles, instead of following Ada into her home office.

Ada stamped the envelopes, wrote her return address on the backs and set them at the edge of her small roll-top desk to be mailed on the 10th of the month. Roberto, Angel, and Mrs. Chabert were on speaking terms now, a good start. She congratulated herself as she walked downstairs and out to the front porch.

She saw Tom sitting on the white wooden rail that connected the two concrete support pillars.

"You're taking a break?"

"Well deserved, I'd say."

"Ada, you took a chance, gave Roberto and the Chabert's a place to start. You were fearless, just as I predicted."

"I didn't think about you during these past few weeks. Would have loved it if you were here, but…"

"Then you don't miss me?"

"Not much."

VITA

Jacqueline Signori has been writing for publication since the age of 10 when a poem entitled "Rain" was printed in a Connecticut state educational magazine in 1957.

She is currently writing a second novel. She is the co-author of one non-fiction book published in 1975, and she has been published in her local newspapers since 1992. In 2001 and 2002, her fiction was published in two anthologies associated with The Prague Summer Seminars, The Prague Summer Program and Charles University in Prague, Czech Republic. She received her MFA in 2003 from the University of New Orleans.

She has been an adjunct faculty member at Kirkwood Community College in Cedar Rapids, Iowa since 2003.

www.ingramcontent.com/pod-product-compliance
Lightning Source LLC
Chambersburg PA
CBHW021130130626
46554CB00002B/938